One Hundred Shining Candles

One Hundred Shining Candles

by
JANET LUNN

illustrated by
LINDSAY GRATER

CHARLES SCRIBNER'S SONS • NEW YORK
Maxwell Macmillan International Publishing Group
New York   Oxford   Singapore   Sydney

First United States Edition 1991

Text copyright © 1990 by Janet Lunn
Illustrations copyright © 1990 by Lindsay Grater

Charles Scribner's Sons Books for Young Readers
Macmillan Publishing Company
866 Third Avenue, New York, NY 10022

Printed and bound in Hong Kong by Everbest
10 9 8 7 6 5 4 3 2 1

Library of Congress Cataloging-in-Publication Data
Lunn, Janet Louise Swoboda, date
One hundred shining candles / Janet Lunn ;
pictures by Lindsay Grater. — 1st U.S. ed.   p.   cm.
"First published in Toronto, Canada, by Lester & Orpen Dennys Limited" — T.p. verso.
Summary: Lucy and Dan make a special gift for their mother at Christmas.
ISBN 0-684-19280-2
[1. Candles — Fiction.   2. Christmas — Fiction.   3. Family life — Fiction.]
I. Grater, Lindsay, ill.   II. Title.   III. Title: 100 shining candles.
PZ7.L979120n   1991   [Fic] — dc20   90-8892

First published in Toronto, Canada, by Lester & Orpen Dennys Limited

For all my grandchildren
JL

hristmas was coming. Snow lay thick on the branches in the deep woods and whitened the log cabins in the clearings.

In the schoolmaster's house, the children were seated on benches and stools, listening spellbound. The schoolmaster was talking about Christmas. But Lucy had stopped listening. For maybe the first time in her ten-year-old life, Lucy, with her tight black braids and her neatly tucked-in collar, was lost in a dream.

"Candles," Mr. Jones had said. "I have seen a hundred candles lighted at one time to celebrate the birth of our Lord. In the big cities I have seen red silk ribbons and dark green cedar festooning the rooms of grand houses. I have seen roast goose and steaming plum puddings set out on long tables. I have seen gifts, wagons and spinning tops and dolls…"

"Please, sir?" It was Dan. "What did the candles look like all lighted?" Lucy was surprised. It wasn't like him to speak out in school. But Dan's blue eyes were shining.

"Oh," − the old man's voice was soft − "the whole room was aglow. There was golden light even in the darkest corners. It was elegant! Most elegant!"

Lucy said nothing to Dan all the way home from school, along the path through the dark forest.

She knew there wouldn't be steaming pudding and roast goose in many cabins in the backwoods of Upper Canada in 1800.

"Maybe some folks in the village might have those things," Lucy thought. But she knew the Jamiesons wouldn't have them. There was no money to spare for celebration, with Ma sick so much of the time and Pa so worried.

"I'm sorry," Pa had told Lucy and seven-year-old Dan. "There will be no presents this Christmas. All we can manage is the bread this year." For as long as Lucy could remember, Ma had baked white bread for Christmas — two loaves — a big one for the family and a small one for the birds. White flour was costly, but when Pa had suggested not having it this year, Ma had said she'd sooner not eat for a week than do without their Christmas bread. Dan had said he'd give his penny for the white flour. Dan was proud of his penny. He called it his fortune and was never without it.

"No, Dan." Pa had been firm. "Grandpa gave you that penny because you were named for him."

Lucy had longed for something like Dan's penny to offer — even if Pa turned it back.

All evening, Lucy was thinking. She was thinking while she cooked the cornmeal stir-about in the big iron pot that hung over the fire. She was thinking while she put away the flax her mother had been spinning and while she tidied up for the night. When, at last, she had finished her chores, she hung her one carefully mended dress on its peg over her bed. And with a smile on her face she lay down to sleep. Because she had a plan, a wonderful, exciting plan.

Pa left early the next morning to walk to the flour mill. He would be away for almost two days. The children went outside to see him off. "If you hear bears or wolves up close, bar the door," he told them. "And you're to mind your ma, and do as you know you ought." Pa nodded at them, turned, and was off through the woods.

Lucy waited until she could no longer hear the crunch of snow under his boots. She grabbed Dan's hand and pulled him over behind the woodpile. "I've got a plan," she whispered, barely able to control her excitement. And she told him about her wonderful idea.

"Candles!" breathed Dan. "It will be light everywhere. It will be light even behind the maple sugar bin, Lucy!"

"And you're not to let on, Dan," Lucy ordered. "It's to be a surprise for Ma's Christmas. I wouldn't have told you except I knew you'd see me making them. You're not to leak out a single word and you're not to give out any of those I-know-a-secret looks either." Lucy's dark eyes were fierce.

"I won't." There was a note of awe in Dan's voice. "I promise. But we'll have to have tallow and wicks to make the candles. Will Pa be angry we took them and didn't ask?"

"Pa's gone, and when he comes back it will be done and he won't know till Christmas. Then he'll be more'n pleased to see Ma so happy." Lucy's voice was so firm Dan dared say no more about Pa.

"Can I help?" he asked.

Lucy didn't want him to help. The candles were her idea, her present. But Dan's blue eyes were so big and so full of longing. She sighed. "Oh, all right. But mind, you've got to be very careful. If you mess it all up, I'll skin you and boil you up for Christmas dinner!"

That evening after school the children sat out on the woodpile wriggling their toes in their thin boots, plotting their candlemaking until their teeth were chattering with the cold and the moon had risen over the big tamarack tree behind the shed. Lucy said Dan could gather the candle frame, the wick, and the tallow from the shed and hide them in the small soap kettle that was kept there.

As for the candles — "They got to be red," they agreed. "Red like the columbine and the sumac," said Dan.

"We'll make them red with Ma's red madder dye," said Lucy. She looked down regretfully at her faded dress. The dye was to have been used for a new red dress in spring.

"I'll fetch it down," Dan offered bravely. The dye crock was in a niche over the fireplace in the cabin.

"No. It was my idea so I'll do the hard part," Lucy declared.

That night Lucy lay in her bed watching the dancing flames in the fireplace make shadows on the dark wall of the cabin and she felt a lot less confident. The shapes looked like herself reaching stealthily towards the niche in the stone chimney. As her fingers closed around it, the shadows grew and became Ma and Pa looking at her reproachfully. She yanked the bedcovers up over her head so she couldn't see the shapes.

She woke at first light and remembered at once what she had to do. She looked across the room. Her mother was still asleep. Swiftly and silently Lucy crept from her bed. She lifted a chair from its place by the table and carried it to the fireplace. She was up on the chair and down again with the dye crock in her hands. She had the chair back in place, the crock under her bed, and was under the covers in a flash. Suddenly she remembered. The tinderbox to light the fire with! Up she jumped! She flew back to the chair, up to the chimney, and was down with the tinderbox and back in bed just as her mother yawned her first yawn.

That afternoon the children raced home from school. They whistled through their chores with such speed that their mother said, "I believe you could raise a barn, just the two of you, if you had a mind to."

Lucy decided they must build the fire behind the house so Ma would not see the smoke. She bustled about, telling Dan what to do. And Dan lugged the logs from the woodpile and the kettle with the candle-making things from the shed. He set the kettle over the logs and, with great ceremony, Lucy lit the fire. In a few moments it was blazing up around the kettle.

"Now stand back, Dan. Not there. Out of the way, over there. Don't you go messing it all up." But it wasn't Dan, serious and intent, who sent their dream up in smoke. It was Lucy with her busying and bossing. When Lucy figured the kettle was good and hot she threw in the lump of tallow and stirred it so hard she knocked the kettle askew. Frantically she tried to straighten it. The kettle tilted. The tallow fell into the fire. Instantly a billow of stinking black smoke rose from the flames.

Horrified, the children stood rooted to the ground. Tears from the smoke ran down their smudged faces.

"I've ruined it," whispered Lucy at last. "I've ruined Christmas." She couldn't even cry, the feeling was so deep and dismal. They sat down on a rock, feeling colder and more miserable than maybe two people have ever felt before or since.

"It ain't ruined, Lucy," Dan said. "I got an idea. I can get some more tallow from Mr. Bosey."

"Mr. Bosey?"

"Remember what Pa said? He said Mr. Bosey would give up his coat for a penny in his pants' pocket. And I've got my penny and I reckon Mr. Bosey will be glad to give me some tallow for my penny."

"No! You can't give up your penny!" Lucy was shocked.

"Yes, I can!" Dan's voice was trembling. "Pa said Grandpa said I was to have something special with my penny and I want us to have candles for Christmas."

Dan ran towards the bay. Mr. Bosey lived on the other side but, because the bay was frozen, it wouldn't take more than fifteen minutes to get there and back.

Lucy knew Mr. Bosey would give Dan the tallow. But Dan's penny would be gone and it was her fault. "I figured I was so almighty fine. But it was me that ruined it after all!"

She was still enveloped by her own bleak feelings when Dan came running back. He thrust a pan of tallow into her hands.

"He wants the pan back, the old skinflint!" Dan was breathless. And he was shining so with his desire to make the candles that Lucy threw her arms around him and hugged him tight. Dan was so surprised that his face turned redder than the madder dye.

And this time they worked together — with great care. Lucy made sure the kettle was steady over the embers of the fire and Dan put the tallow into it.

Like two witches they crouched over their cauldron, watching the white tallow melt and bubble. Then they took the candle frame which Lucy had threaded with five lengths of wick, and Lucy dipped them slowly into the hot tallow. She lifted them out into the cold air so the tallow would harden. She dipped again and again until the candles were almost thick enough. Then it was time to add the color.

"You do it," said Lucy. "You do it because you gave up your penny."

So Dan stirred in the madder dye and dipped the candles once more. He pulled them out.

"Lucy," he wailed. "It won't mix! The candles are all splotchy! They won't be red all over!"

"Hush! You want Ma to hear?" Lucy whispered hoarsely, trying desperately to hide her own disappointment. "Just you go ahead and dunk them candles. Just you dunk and dunk."

So Dan dunked and dunked. When he was finished he held up the candles. They were mottled red and they weren't nearly as straight, either, as the candles Pa made. And there weren't a hundred — only five. Mr. Bosey had only given Dan just that much tallow for his penny.

But Dan and Lucy didn't mind anymore. They scraped the last of the streaky red and white tallow onto their candles with a stick and held them up in the frosty evening air to harden. Then they sat back on their heels and admired their handiwork.

They put out the fire with handfuls of snow. Then, carefully, they placed their candles in the tin box Lucy kept her treasures in — to keep them safe from nibbling mice — and stowed the tin in a chink in the wall of the shed.

The next day Pa came home with two sacks over his shoulders − the big one full of the coarse brown flour the family always used, the small one full of fine white flour for the Christmas bread.

"Here's Christmas," he said tiredly, handing the small sack to Ma. Dan looked at Lucy and quickly looked away again. But he didn't give away their secret.

The day before Christmas Ma baked the Christmas bread, kneading it over and over until it was soft and smooth. She baked it into two delicious-smelling loaves — the small one for the birds and the big one for the family. Together, Lucy and Dan went out and cut a few pine and cedar boughs to lay on the mantel and over the door and window frames.

Finally it was Christmas morning. Fresh snow had fallen in the night, covering the Christmas world with glistening magic.

The children tiptoed from their beds before dawn, even before Pa was up. Outside all was silent with the silence that comes with deep, soft snow. In that silence they set their candles in a row on the table and lit them.

"Ma," Dan called quietly, but their mother was already standing beside him. Pa was right behind her. No one said anything. Lucy turned, suddenly scared, to see what her mother and father were thinking. She saw, in her mother's eyes, the same glowing look she had seen in Dan's eyes when Mr. Jones had told them about the candles. And Pa? Well, Pa's eyes looked wondering and softer than Lucy had seen them since Ma had got sick.

Lucy could contain herself no longer. She took Dan's hand and began to dance around and around the table, telling all about Mr. Jones and the madder-root dye and the spilled tallow and Dan's penny and Mr. Bosey, until everyone began to laugh. And Pa laughed loudest of all. He lifted Dan onto his shoulders, marched him around the room, and said he thought this was surely the best use in all the world a body could put a penny to.

Ma smiled and smiled, and the whole room was bright with the light of a hundred shining candles.